FIVE GET ON THE PROPERTY LADDER

Enid Blyton

FIVE GET ON THE PROPERTY LADDER

Text by
Bruno Vincent

Enid Blyton for Grown-Ups

Quercus

First published in Great Britain in 2017 by

Quercus Editions Ltd
Carmelite House
50 Victoria Embankment
London EC4Y 0DZ

An Hachette UK company

A CIP catalogue record for this book is available
from the British Library

ISBN 978 1 78648 475 8

Text by Bruno Vincent
Original illustrations by Eileen A. Soper
Cover illustration by Ruth Palmer

10 9 8 7 6 5 4 3 2 1

Typeset by CC Book Production

Printed and bound in Germany by GGP Media GmbH, Pößneck

Contents

CHAPTER ONE

Five Feel at Home

After a summer of beach holidays and weddings, Anne, Dick, George, Julian and Timmy were happy to be back in the flat once more, and returning to their old routines. It was comforting to eat dinner together at the kitchen table again, and one evening, as they did so, the conversation turned to something they'd all begun to notice. That – largely as a result of the wedding season – their friends were starting to disappear from the capital.

It all seemed to be gathering pace at the onset of autumn, as people felt they had to get their lives sorted out. The main beneficiaries of London's continuous rental price hike seemed to be the Home Counties, Birmingham, Bristol and Brighton.

'Although, Brighton's getting too pricey for lots of my friends,' George observed. 'Even my mates trying to move to the nice bits of Hastings are finding it a struggle.'

'I don't know why everyone has to rush into these things,' said Anne. 'There's plenty of time, after all . . .'

The others didn't respond. They all suspected that Anne's grand plan was to meet a handsome and handsomely rich man, marriage to whom would absolve her of all financial considerations until he . . . well, that's where their speculations ended.

Dick, George and Julian were less sanguine about their prospects, but were content to stay put for the time being. In fact, after some teething issues in the first year of living together, the household was really starting to gel. It no longer felt that they were shacked up out of convenience; they were truly starting to enjoy it.

Gradually, over the course of the past eighteen months, they had shed some of the old tensions from their childhood. Julian had resolved to be less bossy, Anne to be less helpless and brittle, Dick to be more independent and to drift along through life a little less.

What's more, they were starting to put down local roots – albeit somewhat shallow roots, of the London kind. The cheerful Kurdish lad at the kebab shop now knew Dick, George and Julian's order of choice. The Bangladeshi

Calculations made on the back of an envelope
gave them the sum they had to work with.
It did not make for encouraging reading.

ladies at the post office, formerly quite strict, now smiled at Dick and asked him how he was, in a very auntly fashion, when he went to post the PlayStation games he'd sold online. They knew he always asked for a second-class stamp and no proof of postage.

The homeless man who sat outside the local railway station (until eight p.m., when he picked up his stuff and went home) knew Anne by name (as she knew his – it was Bill), as she always waved and stopped to talk, and if she had no change on her one day, she would give him a bit extra the next.

George had got to know a few dozen of the other dog-walkers in the park. She had progressed beyond being on nodding terms, and was now on hello-saying terms and even (remarkable for her) chatting terms, although conversation never strayed beyond how the dogs were doing, what they ate and so on.

Julian had discovered the cosiest and quietest corner of each pub in succession; he had populated that spot for as long as he could, reading paperbacks in quiet bliss, until gradually he found that everyone knew his name and insisted on being friendly and talking to him. Each time he reached this point, he upped sticks and moved to the next establishment along the High Street, until, with an inward sigh, he came to realize that he had exhausted all the pubs in walking distance, and, rather than drink at home, he would reluctantly be forced to make friends. He was now on three quiz teams.

There were a few other small things that made them feel rooted in this part of north London. They had all signed a petition to reject a planning application for a giant new Sainsbury's – Julian found the idea of a large supermarket nearby incredibly appealing, but the woman who had invited him to sign was blonde, freckly and had a bright, wonky smile that did strange things to his oesophagus. Unable to speak, he had signed. When they heard the proposal was indeed rejected, the housemates had suddenly felt more like a part of the community.

Then there was the suggestion George had made for a new pie at the local pie shop (spinach, onion, rice and tuna – a recipe she had been told by a Russian taxi driver), which had proved so popular it was permanently on the menu. And there was the local newsagent who had found

'What is it?' asked Dick.
'Oh come on, Dick,' said Julian.
'You must have seen them in films. It's a telephone.'

Dick's laptop case (laptop still inside) and returned it to him when he had next gone in, provoking from Dick an uncharacteristically articulate outburst of thanks.

As they talked about all these things over dinner, they agreed they were really starting to feel like they *lived* here.

'What's that sound?' George asked, as a ringing noise broke through the conversation. It didn't sound like anything they knew. It wasn't a smoke alarm, or a ringtone on any of their phones. It wasn't coming through the radio, or (when they all shut up and listened for a moment, and went to the window) from the flats above or below, or the street outside.

It was a trilling bell, clean and insistent. It was not entirely unpleasant to the ear, but it wouldn't stop.

'Woof!' said Timmy.

'I couldn't agree more,' said Julian. 'What the bloody hell *is* it?'

'I think it's coming from down here somewhere,' said Anne, getting on her hands and knees. She started rummaging through the couple of dusty kitchen cupboards that they never used – or rather, in which they had stuffed the rubbish they had no use for, or that belonged to Aunt Fanny and Uncle Quentin (the flat's owners).

As she opened the second cupboard, the ringing became much louder. Everyone gathered round, wondering what it could be. Anne removed a couple of plastic bags from Fenwick's and Peter Jones, filled with lumpy clanking metallic things, and set them aside.

Stuffed down in the corner was a bright red plastic object, with a handset across the top and a circular dial around the front.

'What is it?' asked Dick.

'Oh, come on, Dick,' said Julian. 'You must have seen them in films. It's a telephone.'

'Hello?' said Anne, gingerly holding the receiver up. She coughed, and then wiped the dust off the mouthpiece. 'I'm sorry, say again?' she asked. 'Oh, hello Aunty.'

There was a somewhat anticlimactic sense in the room.

'Why didn't you phone our mobiles?' she asked. She listened. 'No, you wouldn't be using up my free minutes,' she said. 'That's not how it works. You could always text us, or use WhatsA— Pardon?'

Anne turned to the others with a worried look. The suspense that had eased suddenly tightened again. She put her hand over the mouthpiece.

'Bad news,' she said.

CHAPTER TWO

Financial Concerns

'How could they have been so stupid?' Julian asked.

'It's not their fault. They're just not ... financially knowledgeable,' said Anne. 'At least, I imagine. Isn't that right, George?'

'An understatement,' said George. 'What Mummy and Daddy don't know about money, you could ...' She paused. 'Well, they don't know much about money. That's what I'm trying to say.'

'But it's so stupid, so *irresponsible*,' yelled Julian.

'Take it easy, Jules,' said Dick. 'I'm not sure that any of us would be any better.'

'In this day and age!' Julian went on.

'Oh, do *shut up*, Julian,' said Anne. 'It's not helping. We've got things to think about. And lots to do.'

'So what does this mean, exactly, for us?' Dick asked. '*Exactly*?'

FINANCIAL CONCERNS

Dick had asked this question three times now, and each time he had received a perfectly clear answer. But it seemed he was having trouble coming to terms with it.

In light of the renovations that had been necessary to Aunt Fanny and Uncle Quentin's house earlier in the summer (after Uncle Quentin's reckless experiments had blown part of it to smithereens), they had been forced to dip into their savings.

Owing to one thing or another, including Fanny's natural frugality and the handsome pension Quentin had been awarded by G.C.H.Q. for services rendered, they had not had to touch their savings for many years past. And it turned out that the savings were much shallower than they had thought.

This was mainly due to heavy investments in 'heritage' high-street companies, which had yielded steadily for decade after decade, but were now worthless. It seemed that news of the demise of Woolworths and British Home Stores had not reached south Dorset.

'Yes,' Dick said, as George explained this to him once more. 'That does seem a shame. So what?'

'So we've got to move,' said Julian. 'We've got to leave this flat.'

'Right,' said Dick. Then he said, 'What? Why?'

The truth was that Fanny and Quentin were faced with the fact that they only had two assets in the world: Kirrin Cottage, and the flat where Anne, Julian and the others lived. And, in order to rebuild the one, they had to sell the other.

So the housemates had to start looking for somewhere to live.

As they finished dinner, they all tentatively approached the subject of whether they were going to live together again. They were all mightily relieved to find that they all wanted the arrangement to continue.

'God, no, I don't want us to split up,' said Julian. 'I've only just got used to living with you lot. I don't want to have to do that all over again, with a bunch of horrible strangers. Or, rather, I don't want to have to risk inflicting horrible me on a bunch of innocent strangers. Next person I have to get used to living with, as far as I'm concerned, will be Mrs Julesypoos.'

'I wish you wouldn't call yourself that,' said Anne.

It seemed that news of the demise of Woolworths and British Home Stores had not reached south Dorset.

'You'll find yourself saying it in public, sooner or later, and then you'll feel like a wally.'

'I will not feel like a wally,' said Julian with dignity. 'I will feel like a Julesypoos.'

'Fine, do what you like. Right now, we need to find an estate agent.'

CHAPTER THREE

Agent of Doom

Through their generosity, Fanny and Quentin had long allowed their nephews, niece, daughter and her dog to live in their north London flat for considerably below the going rate. This had, unfortunately, allowed the four of them to get used to this cushy scenario and not to plan for if and when it ever came to an end.

Now, they started to search for rental properties online to see how far their money would stretch. Within minutes, they discovered how many properties there were that could accommodate them, including Timmy, and which they could afford: zero.

It was Anne who came up with the solution.

'It would practically be cheaper to buy,' she said.

'Well, why don't we?' asked Julian. 'We've got savings, haven't we?'

'Have we?' asked Dick.

The others weren't at all sure whether they did or did not have savings. Investigation, however, established that they did indeed. There were bits and pieces of money from parents and grandparents that had been squirrelled away. George had an ISA that had been paid for by Quentin; Dick had been given several thousand pounds' worth of Premium Bonds by a godfather on the occasion of his christening, which he had never known about until he asked his parents; Anne had a fair few grand saved from her brief but lucrative stint as a model.

'Quallo,' said Julian. 'And I've got some of my own. Let's pool it and see what we've got!'

Calculations made on the back of an envelope gave them the sum they had to work with. Then they looked at their salaries, and took into consideration the bewildering figures they still had to repay from their student loans. From this, they worked out the most likely figure they would be allowed to borrow. It did not make for encouraging reading.

'But let's see, anyway,' said Anne. 'There's no harm in asking – it can't hurt.'

'Nothing ventured, nothing gained,' said Dick.

'Whoever smelt it, dealt it,' said George.

'To the estate agent!' said Julian.

'Woof!' Timmy agreed.

The four housemates dreaded making contact with an estate agent. They had all had experiences with the breed in the past. The worst part was always trying to get them to talk like a person, and the slightly numbing disappointment you felt when you discovered they were immune to any of the qualities that make someone worth talking to: reason, taste, wit, sensitivity, self-awareness and decency. One always came away from the encounter feeling considerably less human.

But they told themselves that it wasn't fair to judge a whole industry by the few people they had met. They tried to hold out hope that this time it would be different.

Not knowing one estate agent from another, the house-mates simply picked one that wasn't too far away, and that was rather pleasantly located itself. It was on a leafy side-street, set back a little from the road, in a handsome 1930s stucco villa. As they stepped in through the front

'As you can see, it's nice and compact,' Rupert began.
'And full of history. With tonnes of potential to put your own stamp on it.'

door, the four of them felt a little concerned that the establishment might be used to somewhat wealthier clients than they. The office was scattered with breakout spaces between the Nordic designer furniture, a juice bar and (at the back of the room, in a rectangular, plate-glass conservatory) a table-tennis table.

Nevertheless, they introduced themselves to the man behind the nearest desk. Reassuringly, he neglected to throw them out into the street, lock the door and phone the police, in one swift movement. Instead, he listened politely, nodding and saying 'uh-huh' a lot, while making notes on his pad.

'Can I perhaps take your names and contact details first?' he asked.

Anne went first and, when she said her name, the young estate agent looked up and laughed pleasantly.

'Kirrin!' he said. 'What a coincidence! Do you know Rupert Kirrin, then?'

'That unscrupulous swine?' Julian asked. 'Unfortunately, he's our cousin. If you know him, then you have my deepest sympathy, because he's the filthiest, most disreputable lowlife I've ever set eyes up—'

'How delightful to see you all,' said a treacly voice behind them.

They all jumped, and Julian let out a yelp.

'Oh, er – Rupert! What a pleasant surprise,' Julian said. 'I was just saying, ah . . . It's been too long . . .'

'So you guys are looking for a property? Good for you,' Rupert said suavely. 'I'm delighted you've decided to bless us with your patronage. I intend to make sure that you have a fully satisfactory experience . . .'

'Rupert, this really is too much,' said Anne. 'You can't possibly be an estate agent, as well as everything else.'

'Oh, yes, indeed,' said Rupert. 'You know I'm a businessman with a wide-ranging portfolio, and a great deal of that has always involved having a flair for buying and selling property.'

'If you think about it, Anne, he's a natural fit,' said George.

'Yes,' said Anne sadly. 'I'm afraid that's true.'

'Well, now, this isn't any way to talk to our dear cousin,' chuckled Julian. 'If you're offering to personally take over our case, Rupert, old sprout . . .'

'Naturally,' said Rupert. 'If that's all right, Grant?'

'Of course, of course,' said the polite young man.

'Then we'd be terribly grateful to benefit from your expertise,' said Julian, smiling obsequiously.

'Splendid stuff,' Rupert said, already walking away from them. 'Come into my office, and tell me what it is that you're looking for . . .'

CHAPTER FOUR

Warehouse Blues

Rupert listened patiently while George, Julian, Anne and Dick disclosed their desires for a future property. Then he asked about their budget. Then he went quiet and thoughtful for a while, looking out of the window at the office's beautifully manicured garden, across which (several of the housemates noticed, aghast) strutted a peacock.

'Okay,' he said. 'Leave it with me. I'll bring you some great options in no time.'

True to his word, a few days later Rupert phoned to say he had found a terrific place in a part of town that he knew they would be excited about. He came to pick them up in his car, and drove them over to the property.

In their discussions, it had quickly emerged that the housemates' differing personalities meant that they had

She felt pretty sure that the previous occupant had died here, and she wasn't at all convinced they would have been unhappy about it.

very different ideas of the perfect home. Today's property tended towards George's preference.

It was a warehouse in east London, originally built to house an engineering firm specializing in wing parts for aeroplanes. Later, it had been an artist's studio for a couple of decades. For the last twenty years, thanks to a legal dispute, which had recently been resolved, it had stood empty.

'It's certainly a little way off the beaten track,' said Julian, as they drove through the streets of the former manufacturing district.

'It's a very vibrant, up-and-coming area,' Rupert said.

'We'd certainly be very well catered for if we wanted some fried chicken,' said Anne. 'Oh, look – Wyoming Fried Chicken. That's one I've not seen before . . .'

'Fifteen-minute walk to the nearest overground station,' observed Rupert.

'Oh,' said Julian. 'Which one's that?'

'Hackney Wick,' said Rupert.

'Mate, you couldn't get to Hackney Wick by *helicopter* in fifteen minutes,' said Julian. 'We passed it about four miles back.'

'Twenty-minute walk, perhaps,' said Rupert, as he parked up. They all got out.

'I've been to parties around here,' said George. 'Oh, hey, Sam.' She waved at a handsome Japanese youngster who was ambling past.

'You moving here?' Sam asked.

'Thinking of it, maybe,' said George.

'Lol,' said Sam, and, with a wave, ambled away.

'That young man is stoned,' said Julian.

'That young man is a forty-year-old woman,' George pointed out.

'That's no excuse,' said Julian.

'Let's have a look at the place, shall we?' Rupert asked.

When Rupert had shown them round the dusty, empty warehouse, George was trying to understand her own profound disappointment. What was it, exactly, that she'd expected? It was a warehouse that needed to be converted from a warehouse into a living space. Warehouses – pre-conversion – were not notorious for their homely atmosphere and cosiness.

'Lots of space, light and airy,' Rupert said, walking ahead

of them. 'People are going crazy for the industrial-chic thing, these days. And an easily maintained garden . . .'

He beckoned George forward to see the outside space. George tried the door to find it refused to open all the way – the fence was too close. She peered out of the window instead and saw a narrow stretch of concrete.

'You can't even get out of the door, Rupert; there's not enough room,' she said.

'As I said, very easily maintained.' He turned to talk to the others, who were examining the interior. 'Obviously, you'll have to clean, and rewire, and then properly build partitions for the bedrooms,' said Rupert. 'But it's straightforward work.'

'I don't know what this artist was on,' said Julian. 'Just look at this installation.' He gazed dolefully at one corner, where there was a pile of detritus made from dead rat carcases, mouse turds, pigeon feathers and litter.

'I just do not understand modern art,' he said.

'That's not art,' said George.

'No, well – ha,' said Julian. 'I couldn't have put it better myself.'

26

'I . . . Never mind,' she said. She looked at the warehouse around her with frank disgust. 'So this is within our budget, is it?'

'Nearly,' said Rupert.

'"Nearly"?' asked Dick. 'I mean, surely it is, or it isn't?'

'It practically is,' Rupert said.

'Meaning what exactly?' George asked.

'Meaning that I know the owner is in a bit of trouble and motivated to sell. The market price isn't the selling price, if the owner is desperate. So, if you offer what you told me your budget is, there's a small chance that they'll accept.'

'How small?' George asked.

Rupert pretended to think about it for a moment. 'Very small,' he said.

'So, really, what you're saying is that the price of this place is well outside our budget.'

'As your budget stands, yes.'

'What do you mean, "as our budget stands"?' George asked. 'Why would our budget change?'

'People often find they can stretch to more money when they find a property they love. I think, if that happens, you

'So this . . .' Anne said. She refused to call it a house.
'This . . . place.'

might find some elasticity in your finances. Do I take it that that . . . *hasn't* happened here?'

George cast another look around the warehouse. It certainly aroused plenty of feelings in her, but love was not one of them.

'It would cost thirty grand to get this place ready for habitation,' she said. 'Even in the most basic way. I mean, you'd have to build the bedrooms, for a start.'

'I'd say you'd need to double that figure, at least,' said Rupert.

'So what the hell are we doing here,' George asked, 'if we can't even afford to buy it, let alone the other costs? You may as well take us to look at the Emirates Stadium and ask if our budget can stretch to that!'

'You don't like it,' said Rupert. 'I'm getting that. It doesn't speak to you.'

The message had finally sunk in. The empty, gloomy warehouse, which bore no single visible sign of former human occupation, was not speaking to them. Nor could they imagine it speaking to anyone, except possibly a rat who had fallen out of love with life and was looking for a private spot to do away with himself.

'Don't worry,' said Rupert. 'I've got other options coming thick and fast. You leave it with me.'

'If that's that, then let's leave,' said Anne, covering her nose. 'I'll smell of dead pigeons for the rest of the day as it is, and I'm sure there's a risk of infection.'

'You know what, I think I get it now,' said Julian, leaning over the pile of trash. He smiled and nodded. 'Yes,' he said. 'Yes! When you think about it, it's really rather clever . . .'

'Come *on*, Julian, for God's sake!' yelled George from the door.

CHAPTER FIVE

Five Go Cottaging

It wasn't long before Rupert contacted them again, with another hopeful property. He picked them up one evening after work and drove them once more – this time not into the city, but out. They wound their way into the suburbs, past quiet streets, where nice ordinary people lived their pleasant, normal lives. Then the suburbs themselves began to thin out, and were interspersed with larger patches of green.

The house they were travelling to was much more to Anne's specifications. Imagining the ideal home, she instinctively thought of an old-fashioned cottage in the countryside, bathed in hot sunshine and surrounded by flowers and a tall hedge. She pictured a thatch, but not only was it expensive and a flagrant fire hazard, she'd also heard that thatches were infested by dozens of species of insects, birds and vermin. So she was willing to consider a tiled roof – preferably wobbly – and casement windows, with the panes in a latticed pattern.

Anne looked at the picture Rupert had handed her as his car weaved down the little lanes, and her heart fluttered. It was very close to what she wanted. There was a garden, enclosed by a fence, and the house was picturesquely timbered. Timber was more or less equal to thatch in picturesqueness. Having one certainly cancelled out not having the other.

Was it possible? she wondered. Could she really own (or co-own, or part-co-own) and live in such a house?

Rupert's car slowed, and crawled into the drive.

Everyone remained silent as they got out. They were waiting for Rupert to speak first, and explain. But he didn't, and instead ambled towards the front door.

'Are you going to ask permission to park in their drive-way?' Anne asked. 'While we go to look at the cottage?'

But, instead of answering, he took out a key, unlocked the door and went inside. Anne followed him with a hot sensation rising in her chest. The picture of the cottage trembled in her hand.

'This can't be it,' she said quietly.

'I'm sensing you don't feel this one is quite
right for you,' Rupert said.
'It,' said Julian, 'is a shithole.'

'As you can see, it's nice and compact,' Rupert began. 'And full of history. With tonnes of potential to put your own stamp on it. I think this could be a really great space.'

'It's *horrible*!' Anne shrieked.

The building in which they stood was a dingy bungalow with a flat, tarmacadamed roof. There was thick brown carpet throughout, which was almost invisible beneath a matt of cat hair, and every room was decorated with pale orange 1970s wallpaper, adorned with a jazzy pattern that reminded Julian of the neon fireworks he experienced across his retinas at the onset of a migraine.

'What's this?' Anne asked, thrusting the photograph at Rupert.

Rupert nodded at the wall, where, Anne saw with a gasp, there hung the self-same photograph.

'Why did you show me this?' she asked. 'Where's that house? That's the one I want to see!'

'You *are* seeing it,' said Rupert. 'And, if you lived here, you could see it every day. I just wanted to show you an example of the impressive decorative aspects on offer.'

'They've certainly impressed me,' said Julian. 'Very strongly.'

'Is there a garden?' asked George.

'Certainly,' said Rupert. He reached to draw the lace curtain aside, but it came off in his hand. He discreetly dropped it behind the wicker armchair that stood nearby.

'Wow,' said George.

'"Wow" is right,' said Rupert. 'I'm glad you can see the potential.'

The garden appeared to have been allowed to grow unchecked since the Second World War. Brambles, grass, weeds and all sorts of plants had climbed three-quarters of the way up the window, reaching above head height.

'I've never seen such potential,' said Julian. 'It has nothing except potential.'

'I'm delighted you agree,' said Rupert. 'So, what do you think of this charming little pied-à-terre?'

Four faces turned towards him, showing variations on a theme of despair and horror. Timmy's tail hung still.

'I'm sensing you don't feel this one is quite right for you,' Rupert said.

'It,' said Julian, rolling the words around his mouth like vintage port, 'is a *shit*hole.'

Anne flicked a tear out of one corner of her eye with

her finger. She violently wanted to let Rupert know what she thought of him for this despicable trick. But, inwardly, she knew that any attempt would be doomed to fail. The man was shameless. Besides, there were more urgent and crucial facts to consider.

'So, this . . .' Anne said, and stopped to try to get control of her voice. She refused to call it a house. 'This *place*,' she said. 'Is this . . . ? Please tell me it's within our budget.'

'It nearly is,' said Rupert. 'Very nearly.'

'Are you still holding out hope that we're going to find extra money somewhere?' George asked. 'After everything we've said to you?'

'Perhaps Fanny and Quentin might be persuaded to help?' Rupert suggested.

'They're utterly boracic, mate,' said Julian. 'That's what got us into this bind in the first place.'

'Ah,' said Rupert. 'And there are no other potential avenues to explore?'

'When we pooled all our money to see what we had, we didn't leave out a chunk of it,' said George. 'We added up everything. That's what "how much we can afford" means.'

'I've never seen such potential,' said Julian.
'It has nothing except potential.'

'You'd be amazed what you can find, if you really try,' Rupert said.

'Be that as it may,' said Anne, with her eyes shut, 'as things stand, even *this* place is beyond our means?' She opened her eyes and cast another dispirited look round it again. It was so dismal and hopeless. She felt pretty sure that the previous occupant died here, and she wasn't at all convinced they would have been unhappy about it.

Rupert nodded. 'As things stand,' he said. 'I'm afraid so.'

'What does that leave us?' Dick asked. He hardly dared to guess.

'Let me look,' said Rupert. 'I'm sure I'll find something. Leave it to me. I know I'll find you something . . .'

'I'm going to start using the word "potential" the way he uses it,' said Julian, as they left. 'I love it. It's like he's taken the concept of language, broken it, and then used it as a weapon against itself . . .'

'I'm sorry to say this, Rupert . . .' said George. 'Actually, I'm not. I'm afraid this relationship has broken down. I think it's time we started seeing other estate agents.'

'Woof,' agreed Timmy.

CHAPTER SIX

Five Barge In

Although it was high up on their to-do lists, none of them made an immediate move to find a new estate agent. Therefore, when Julian received a call from Rupert the following week, saying that he had another property they might be interested in, Julian reluctantly listened. Naturally, they viewed the prospect of a new Rupert recommendation with cold hostility.

'What did *he* want?' asked Anne, as Julian put down the phone. But the expression of sarcasm Julian had assumed at the beginning of the conversation had dissipated. In fact, he looked intrigued.

'I think it might be worth looking at, you know,' he said. 'He's just sent through a picture. Have a look at this . . .'

They all gathered round, and their expostulations of disbelief died on their lips. Timmy jumped up, trying to get a look. There was a thoughtful silence.

'Woof?' asked Timmy.

George turned to look at him.

'It doesn't look too awful,' she admitted. She showed him the photograph.

'Woof!' Timmy agreed. However, he said it just to please her, and because he trusted her judgement. The photo was, to him, just a bleary smudge.

Having investigated Anne and George's preferred types of housing, and found them impossible, Rupert was now focusing on Dick's suggestion. And, in fact, it seemed he might have struck gold.

'Let's get this straight, right from the beginning,' said George, as they all got out of the train together. They had travelled about twenty miles north of London, and there was a bit of a walk from the station. 'This *is* within our price range? We *could*, in theory, afford this?'

'Yes,' Rupert said. 'In fact, your collected savings mean that you could buy it for cash. It's obviously not a freehold or a leasehold. But it's a substantial investment and a property where you could live and, I think, potentially be very happy.'

They had been walking down a country path as he said this, Timmy running ahead of them and back, barking happily about what he had found. Now they came out alongside a canal, which stretched off into the distance in both directions.

It was an auspiciously timed visit. The weather, which had been dreary all week, had suddenly cleared, making for a bright, warm, rosy autumn evening. There was a hint of barbecuing sausages in the air, no doubt from one of the barges nearby. As they walked along the towpath, insects buzzed in the air and birds sang to each other. It was as though summer hadn't suddenly stopped, but was instead drifting happily away into the sunset, thought Julian. Like these boats, in fact.

The first few barges they walked past did not excite jealousy. Paint had peeled, woodwork rotted, windows had become grimily opaque from lack of cleaning. One proprietor leant over the edge of his boat, untying a tow rope with a grimace. He looked about seventy, with thin, wiry arms and a bulging pot belly. They bid him a cheery hello, which he answered with a suspicious stare and a cough through his roll-up.

Beyond this was a boat that seemed long-abandoned, with cracked windows and empty beer cans thrown on the roof. The four housemates began to entertain dark thoughts about Rupert's propensity to lie via the medium of photography. But he kept walking past that one, briskly.

The next boat, however, was a revelation. There were plant pots along the roof, tended with minute care into a mini-allotment of sorts – Anne spotted a tomato plant and a selection of herbs. A trail of smoke rose from the chimney and, at one end of the boat, there were several happy young people.

This was where the smell was coming from. One of the men had a small barbecue, on which he was cooking sausages, while the woman next to him was preparing wraps, with salad and sauce, for the sausages to go in. It made the stomach rumble. As the housemates and Rupert walked past, a second young woman emerged from inside, holding beers for the others.

'Where's Rich?' asked the first woman.

'Reading,' said the second.

Julian peered in through the window and saw a young man resting on a cot, his feet up on the end of the bed,

'I'm afraid this relationship has broken down.
I think it's time we started seeing other estate agents.'

paperback in hand, bathed in sunshine. A thrill ran through him like the ringing of a bell.

'Hello!' said Anne.

The boat people turned, smiled and waved, and asked whether it was 'the blue boat' they were coming to look at. Once more, the housemates faltered. The boat in the picture was indeed blue, but they were never sure of anything where Rupert was concerned.

'It is,' said Rupert.

'Oh, good for you!' said the first woman. 'I'd love to have that. Hope you get it!'

This heartened them considerably, and they pressed on. Not much further along, they caught sight of the barge. Perhaps their previous dealings with Rupert had lowered their expectations; perhaps it was the sun glinting off the beautifully polished blue exterior or the gentle, warm and peaceful countryside that surrounded them, but their hearts all swelled at the sight of it.

'Woof!' yelled Timmy, rushing forward.

'Careful, Timmy!' said George, but he ignored her and leapt from the towpath on to the foredeck.

'Let's have a look inside, shall we?' asked Rupert. And,

climbing on with a great deal of care for his expensive suit, he unlocked the door.

'The owner's given this up with huge reluctance,' Rupert explained, 'because he met a girl on one of the other boats, and they're moving in together – on to her boat.'

'*Ahhhh*,' said Anne. 'Isn't that *lovely*? Don't you think, George?' Anne only occasionally made the mistake of trying to appeal to George's womanly instincts, and instantly realized what she had done. George flared her nostrils, and showed no other signs of having heard.

'There's plenty of space,' said Dick, clambering down the stairs. 'I wouldn't have thought a boat could fit four people . . .'

'Woof!' said Timmy.

'. . . and a dog,' Dick added. 'Sorry, Timmy.'

Rupert walked through the boat, delivering what was, they assumed, a stream of jargon, spin and outright false-hood. The phrase 'deceptively spacious' floated back to them. But they weren't listening. All five were lost in their own reverie.

Anne could see at a glance that the previous owner had been male. And, in the same glance, she saw, too, the myriad possibilities he had overlooked for prettification and making cosy. The wooden floor needed sanding and re-varnishing, and possibly a nice rug. A framed picture here or there wouldn't go amiss. Well-chosen material for little curtains (which she would enjoy making) could make the windows look perfectly adorable. And she would never tire of explaining to men that lampshades were not a gratuitous luxury. And perhaps a nicely patterned shower curtain . . . a few plants . . . She could really fall in love with turning this into a place for others to fall in love with.

George was always interested in a form of living that was outside the obvious and mainstream. The idea of being on a boat – and this boat, in particular – appealed to her hugely, even though she had never thought of living on one before. What's more, Timmy seemed thrilled with the place and had already gone for a swim, shaken himself dry and set off at a sprint into the undergrowth to terrorize the local wildlife.

Julian's pretentions were flattered by the romance of the place. And it really wasn't so small, when you looked at it. After all, hadn't they all lived for weeks, and even months, in tiny tents, and had a whale of a time? They thrived in places like this. It wouldn't be forever, it would no doubt be an adventure and they would be sure to meet lots of interesting people. He felt convinced it would be something they looked back on with great joy. And it might prove an inspirational place to finish writing his novel . . .

Dick was stunned that his housemates had all fallen in with his suggestion so swiftly. He liked the sensation of being on a boat, and the freedom of it – of not being tied down to one particular place, except in the strictly literal sense that you *did* have to tie a barge to one particular place most of the time.

Rupert was beaming. 'I knew this would strike a chord,' he said. 'In fact, I was so confident, I brought some champagne . . .'

They sat at the front of the barge and celebrated. The bottle allowed just enough for one glass each. None of them had had dinner, and so the bubbles went rather to their heads.

By the time they'd drunk their glass, and were feeling that a single bottle of champagne doesn't stretch very far, the inhabitants of the next barge came along to investigate. Dick, Anne, George and Julian were delighted and,

'There's plenty of space,' said Dick. 'I wouldn't
have thought a boat could fit four people . . .'

determined not to miss this opportunity to make new friends, they asked if there was a pub nearby.

There was.

Julian and the others rather expected Rupert to disapprove, and insist they go back to town. But, in fact, it turned out his wife had given him the evening off childcare and, to their surprise, he seemed eager to get involved.

They soon discovered that Rupert was one of those public-school boys who sees everything as a competition that he has to win, and, what's more, refuses to admit that he's drunk too much. In order to show how disgustingly wealthy he was, he also insisted on paying for everything.

The fellow bargers, who had introduced them to the pub, showed no less enthusiasm for drinking, and, in the jollity of their meeting one another, no one noticed what a steep alcoholic descent they were making.

'I'm sure it's okay,' said Rupert woozily, as they unlocked the barge to get back on. They had been invited on to the others' barge, but it wasn't big enough for all of them, so they were all piling on to the blue boat.

'Just be careful,' said Rupert.

Julian put down the crate of ciders that he had brought

from the pub. Anne dropped one of the glasses she was taking out of a cupboard.

'I'm sure that's okay,' said Rupert. 'Let's just be careful. I'm going to rest my eyes for a moment. Be careful,' he said again, over the sound of a second breaking glass.

Dick and George marvelled at how soundly Rupert was able to sleep in an enclosed space full of roaring noise. Everyone was now, to a lesser or greater extent, blotto, and soon enough someone was smoking a cigarette. A speaker had been brought over from the other boat and loud music was blaring, while George and Dick were playing a rowdy game of liar's dice with their new friends. Julian found it impossible to hear what anyone was saying without sticking his head directly in front of the mouth of his conversant.

Then suddenly peace of a sort descended, when everyone noticed that someone's cigarette had set fire to some bed linen. In trying to flap it about to put it out, Dick managed to start fires in two or three other places. The barge filled with smoke, and emptied of people.

Julian charged around the place drunkenly, trying to find a bucket. When he did, he saw that the flames had grown so wildly that a bucket was quite useless to combat them. There was, in fact, a strange beauty to it all, he thought. At this point, there was a loud crack, and he felt water gurgling around his ankles. It contrasted with the scorching heat wonderfully, and he splashed about in it for a few moments, before noticing the screaming voices from outside. He clambered out to see what was going on, and was roughly grabbed by Rupert's strong arms and hauled to safety.

They all watched from the towpath as the inside of the boat churned with fierce orange flames, vomiting columns of black smoke. The barge suddenly listed as the smoke contended with a furious explosion of steam, and then, with a few gigantic gulps, the drama of the spectacle faded, and the barge came to rest on the floor of the canal. Only the top of its roof peeped miserably from the water.

'I *did* say be careful,' said Rupert, newly sober.

'Woof,' said Timmy.

CHAPTER SEVEN

Damage Limitation

If there was anything more brutal than waking up with a bitter hangover to discover one has done thousands of pounds' worth of damage, Julian couldn't imagine what that would be. When awakening in what he described as his 'shame well', he was usually one to run away from any bad behaviour of the previous evening and hide from it for as long as possible. But this new situation was of a different magnitude, and in fact it wouldn't help to do anything but acknowledge the truth.

Still, he wasn't exactly in a rush to face up to things. He sat at the kitchen table, shivering with shock and self-loathing, nibbling at a piece of toast and marmite, and watching his cup of tea go cold. He was prepared for lifelong debt, prison and public humiliation. He kept glancing at his phone, trying to summon up the courage to ring Rupert.

'Are we going to prison?' asked Dick, from the door-way.

Julian looked up at him disconsolately. 'I don't know,' he said. 'Maybe.'

George, who was lying on the sofa with a cushion over her head, groaned.

'Won't we be allowed to pay it back?' Dick asked.

'I don't know,' Julian said again. 'Maybe.'

'Rupert said the barge cost almost exactly what we had in savings,' Dick said. 'If we paid for it, that would clean us out. And just after we'd found a great place, too.'

'Please don't,' said George. 'Just let me die in peace.'

'Did something bad happen last night?' asked Anne, walking in. She saw their faces and realized that something bad *had* happened.

Julian's phone buzzed and, looking at it, he flinched.

'Rupert,' he said.

The name seemed to make some connection in Anne's brain. She went white, clutched her face in her hands and ran from the room.

Julian picked up on the second ring and announced himself with a caveman's grunt.

They tidied up with all the rigour of the still hungover.

'Rupert, here,' said a bright voice.

'I'm sorry,' croaked Julian. 'I'm so sorry.'

'Ah! Dear cousin. Not to worry – people miss appointments all the time. Can't be helped.'

Julian cleared his throat. 'I beg your pardon?'

'Happens to everyone. Please don't concern yourself.'

'Hwah?'

'Although, I'm afraid I've got some sad news,' Rupert glided on. 'The property we were going to see yesterday was, unfortunately, vandalized in the night. Beyond repair, I'm sorry to say. Awful business. Local youths, the other barge inhabitants seem to agree. I spoke to the occupants of a nearby boat, but apparently they were sound asleep and heard nothing. Still, it's in the hands of the insurers now, so hopefully no one will be out of pocket.'

Julian held the phone away from his face and looked at it, blinking. When he put it back to his ear, Rupert was still talking.

'. . . a terrible shame; I was sure you and the others would have loved the boat.'

Julian's booze-dumbfounded brain was slowly catching up. He felt as though he was soaring upwards on some unexpected paradisal draught, from the depths of hell, up to his former habitat – mere maudlin despondency. He had almost never felt such an improvement.

He choked back a yell of thanks and admiration.

'Well,' he said, with difficulty. 'I'm . . . sorry to hear that. Dreadful shame. And, er . . . thanks for accepting my apology.'

'Think nothing of it, dear old bean,' said Rupert. 'And now, if you'll excuse me, I have a pressing engagement. Yes, officer, please sit down; thank you so much for coming; this won't take a minute of your time . . . Speak soon, Julian,' he said, and disconnected.

Julian's heart throbbed with conflicting emotions. He felt like a skulking villain, yet he also felt excoriating relief, and gratitude. In his guilt, he had of course forgotten how many scurrilous and underhand situations his devious cousin had talked his way out of over the years. It was second nature to him. He was practically a supervillain.

Julian decided to break the good news to the others.

They all had the the same reaction – sincere relief marbled with dark guilt.

But it also meant, in property terms, they were back at square one.

Even when they were more or less recovered from their physical frailties, they still felt emotionally drained. But they knew there was no time to hang about – estate agents were due to show prospective buyers around the flat in the next few days. It had to be cleaned, and they had to get out. But, for the time being, they didn't feel up to rousing themselves from the settee in front of the television.

As the third gardening programme in a row came on screen, George said gloomily, 'If it carries on like this, we'll have to go and live on my plot of land.'

'I'm not sure I could live on Kirrin Island permanently, George,' said Anne. 'It's just not convenient.'

'Not that one,' she said. 'I mean my one in Scotland.'

Julian was only half listening, but he now put the television on mute. Slowly, the other three all turned to look at George.

'Woof?' asked Timmy.

'Oh,' she said. 'Didn't I tell you about that?'

They stared.

'It's nothing, really,' she said. 'It's just a hundred square yards of pasture or something. You couldn't live on it. Or off it, either.'

'You'd be surprised what I can and can't do,' said Julian. 'I like a challenge. You *own* this?'

'Yeah,' George said. 'It was part of a charity project, to protect this ancient wood that the council wanted to chop down. People bought hundred-yard patches of it for a few hundred quid, to make sure it didn't get destroyed.'

'Sounds idyllic,' said Anne.

'It's just earth,' George said. 'There's nothing there.'

'I'm sick of looking at properties in and around London, only to find out we can't afford them,' said Julian.

'I'll second that,' said Dick. 'And it seems that, while a barge has its charms, it isn't quite as . . . er . . . secure as we'd like.' No one else dared add a comment to this.

'So maybe a weekend in Scotland to look at this place is in order?' Anne asked.

'Woof!' agreed Timmy.

CHAPTER EIGHT

Off the Road

That weekend, there were many viewings of their own flat, and so the four housemates decided to grasp the nettle (or the thistle) and head up to Scotland straight away. They tidied up with all the rigour of the still hungover, which involved cramming all the rubbish into one cupboard, brushing the crumbs off the kitchen table and replacing the light bulb in the bathroom with a dimmer wattage. Then they investigated hiring a car that could take all of them, including Timmy, and then, seeing how much it would cost, abandoned the plan and borrowed a friend's instead.

There was always something jolly about setting off on a journey like this. Timmy, as always, nestled on his blanket in the boot for a nice lengthy nap; Anne sat in the front seat with the *A to Z* propped open on her lap (this car did not boast a satnav); George put on her driving sunglasses and plugged her iPhone into the stereo; Dick and Julian sat in the back seats, and settled at once into their childhood roles of aggravating each other.

'Ow! George! Julian pinched me!'

Anne and George looked out at the sunny scenery – at least, what was visible beyond the M1 – and smiled serenely.

'Dick, those are *my* Everton mints, you little bastard.'

'George, can I go to the toilet?'

'I'll bang your heads together!' shouted Anne suddenly. The two boys lapsed into silence.

'That's *disgusting*,' said Julian, at length. 'Dick's farted!'

'I've done no such thing. It's the dog.'

'Timmy?' asked George from the front seat. 'Was that you?'

A guilty silence was all the answer she received.

'I thought as much,' George said. 'I can smell 'em a mile off.'

'Well,' said Anne quietly, 'if you fed him *dog* food, perhaps you wouldn't have to . . .'

'*Please* can we stop to go to the toilet?' Dick asked. 'I really need to go. Also, Julian's not sharing his sweets . . .'

'Ow! George! Julian pinched me!'
'Dick, those are my Everton mints, you little bastard.'
'I'll bang your heads together!' shouted Anne.

Seeing a services up ahead, George sighed and flicked on the indicator.

Dick came back from the service station, arms laden with crisps and sweets. He also had coffees for everyone, a bag of pastries, and several magazines. He was smiling from the effort of blanking out the amount of money he had just spent.

'You got *Total Film*?' said Julian. 'I haven't read that in ages. More of a *Sight and Sound* man, myself, of course.'

'*Total Film* is for me. I got the latest *Fat Smelly Bastard Monthly* for you,' said Dick through a mouthful of Wine Gums. 'It's somewhere in the pile.'

'I wonder if they've printed my letter,' said Julian. As he thumbed through the magazines, the engine started up and they were on their way again.

Peace reigned for three and a half minutes.

'Dick, can I have a Chocolate Eclair, please?'

'No.'

'I don't know why you eat those things, anyway,' Julian said. 'They're revoltingly oversweet.'

'Good. You don't have to eat them.'

'Can't I just have *one*?'

'No.'

'But I'm hungry.'

'Well, you've got your Everton mints, haven't you?'

'I finished those.'

'What does that matter to me?'

'Ugh,' Julian sighed. 'What if I was dying of starvation?'

'Immediately after eating a family-sized bag of Everton mints?' Dick flicked over a page in his magazine. He sighed. 'Why is M. Night Shyamalan still allowed to make movies? It just doesn't make sense.'

'Apparently, the last two are quite good,' said Julian, reading over his shoulder.

'Oh, really?' Dick asked. 'I stopped watching them, like, five films ago.'

'Yeah, apparently,' said Julian. 'Quite good, I heard.'

'Well,' said Dick, 'there you go.'

'Hmm,' said Julian.

They listened to the buzz and swoosh of the motorway.

Without tilting his head, Julian ran his eyes over Dick's stash of sweets, and his intently reading face. He looked out of the window for a moment, and then, as though an interesting thought had just struck him, he turned to his brother and asked, 'Hey, Dick, could I have a Chocolate Eclair?'

'No.'

'George!' said Julian. 'Dick's being selfish.'

'We've got another eight hours of this,' said George, with chilling quietness. 'I will literally break both of your noses, kick you in the balls and leave you on the hard shoulder, if you keep this up.'

Julian opened his mouth to protest, then thought better of it. Instead, he raised his eyebrows and looked out of the window with an expression of innocence. He looked at the Christopher Isherwood paperback in his hand; this was valuable reading time, if only reading didn't make him carsick. He picked his nose, tried to flick the rolled up bogies out of the window, and watched trees flashing past until they made him dizzy.

'This music isn't bad,' he said, laying his head back and starting to doze.

'I'm aware of that,' said George.

Timmy, in the boot, found himself wondering why exactly humans insisted on trying to live together – they never even smelled each others' bum. None of the dogs he knew acted like this. He yawned, and settled down for a kip.

'Left,' said Anne. 'Then left again.'

George accelerated down the bumpy track.

'Now, another left,' said Anne.

George followed her instructions, until they came to a turning.

'Where now?' George asked.

Anne peered at the map, looked up at the road, and then down at the map again.

'Left,' she said.

'We can't go left *again*,' George said. 'We'll go in a square!'

'What do you want me to tell you?' Anne asked. 'It's what the map says.'

'There's not even any road through here,' George protested.

'I think that's because we've arrived . . .' Anne said. 'It should be just over this hill . . .'

George's heart quickened. Her own little plot of land,

right here. Not Kirrin Island, which she'd been given, but this place, which she had bought – and for sound environmental reasons, too.

The car, which was very much not engineered for cross-country terrain, bumped violently over every dried lump of turf, prompting cries of shock from everyone except George, who, with difficulty, kept her hands fixed to the juddering steering wheel.

'Keep it down, you moaning sons of bitches,' said George, in tremolo. 'I'm doing my best – ah!'

She braked. Everyone came back to rest on their seats with a gasp (and a dog's yelp), and breathed.

'Here we are,' said George. She surveyed the sight ahead of her with a sigh of satisfaction.

The ancient woodland, with its charitable protected status, stretched out in front of them. The trees were widely spaced enough for the car to pass through, although George suddenly had misgivings about actually driving on to the land.

'I don't think we've got much choice,' said Anne, now consulting the map which detailed George's specific plot of land. 'The whole point is that this land we're on, now, belongs to the farmer who's attempting to sell it. In fact, we're told specifically not to trespass on it, if at all possible.'

'Forward, then,' said George, booting up the motor. A further few minutes of yelping and groaning and bouncing across hard furrows followed, until (with Anne following precise directions on the map, as close as possible to the nearest yard) they came to rest on the actual strip of land.

Dick and Julian had eaten their final batch of crisps and sweets over the past hour, and were now suffering sharp sugar crashes. Climbing out of the car, they felt pudgy and lethargic.

'What are we doing here, again?' Julian asked.

'Just seeing the land,' said George. 'Seeking encouragement. Taking in the scenery. Where does it extend to, anyway, Anne?'

Anne had been peering closer and closer at the map, and cross-referencing with the G.P.S. data on her phone. She looked up at them and frowned distractedly, and then concentrated again on map and phone. When she surveyed the scene again, her frown had settled into one of firm disappointment.

'Timmy?' asked George. 'Was that smell you?'
A guilty silence was all the answer she received.

'Erm,' she said. 'How large was this plot, did you say, George?'

'Hundred square yards,' said George. She looked around her at the pine forest, smelled the fresh mountain air, looked at the fast-descending sun and then at the earth nearabout, wondering which patch was hers. If they pitched their tents here, she thought, there might be some food they could forage. Roots, weeds and nuts – and maybe Timmy would catch them a rabbit. Hopefully, they could build a small fire and warm up something from the picnic basket, if Dick and Julian hadn't eaten everything.

'Hmm,' said Anne thoughtfully. 'You know, when a number has double apostrophes after it, it means measured in inches, right? And one apostrophe means feet. Am I correct?'

'How do they measure yards, then?' asked George with interest, looking over her shoulder.

'That may be academic. Look here.'

'It's not a *Spinal Tap* situation, I hope,' muttered Julian.

'I hope not,' said Dick. 'Nearest hospital can't be for twenty miles.'

Julian tutted and raised his eyes to heaven. Anne, however, had seen *Spinal Tap*, and knew what he meant.

'Well,' she said, diplomatically, 'the plot's not measured in *inches*, at least.' She turned from the map to the other documentation George had given her. 'But there's no mention of yards here, either.'

'What?' asked George, snatching the letter out of her hand. 'Let me read this.'

She read it. She took two deep breaths, then read it again. 'Hmm,' she said.

'Woof?' asked Timmy.

'Well may you ask, Timmy,' said George.

As someone who always tended to expect the worst, on the lengthy drive up, George had quite uncharacteristically allowed herself to fantasize about this moment. She had pictured a sylvan glade, or a stretch of empty forest, in which they all might . . . well, 'frolic' would be going too far. But running through it, while being chased by Timmy and laughing, had, temporarily, entered her mind. Obviously, they did not own it in the sense that they could build on it, or even camp on it, for more than a few days, without being told to move on; the conditions of purchase meant she was allowed to come and set eyes on it, no more.

But now she saw the undeniable evidence of her foolishness. She had not purchased a hundred square yards of forest, but a hundred square feet. And that meant a plot which was ten feet long and ten feet wide – scarcely large enough to pitch a tent on. In fact, assuming they had parked correctly, George's patch of land was only just large enough to fit the car, and all five of them, so long as they were standing up.

The whole point of this journey was to pitch camp on land that was actually *theirs*, so they could rid themselves of these twin feelings of hopelessness and homelessness, just for one night. And, unless they wanted to leave this car (which was not theirs) on property that was also not theirs, and risk God knew what, this plan of camping was now out of the window.

Looking at Anne, George saw that she had realized this too. She decided to let Anne explain it to her brothers, while she went and threw a stick for Timmy – they both might as well stretch their legs before getting back into the car for an all-night drive, and, after all, here he was, panting in front of her, with a fat branch in his jaws.

'Okay, go and fetch *that*, you beast,' she said, flinging it into the distance with all her might. She trotted after him, threw it again when he returned, and repeated the exercise half a dozen times until the car was far behind her. She had walked perhaps half a mile when she threw the stick over the brow of a hill, and heard a clunk, followed by an angry shout. She quickened her pace, hoping she hadn't assaulted an innocent farmer.

Instead, as she crested the hillock, she saw a man in a hard hat and high-vis jacket, standing next to a bulldozer and holding the stick. Timmy was jumping around in excitement for him to throw it, but he was staring at the lump of tree with bewilderment.

'Timmy!' George said. 'Come back here, and calm down. I'm *so* sorry about that,' she went on, to the man. 'I really had no idea you were there. Honestly.'

He regarded her suspiciously as she approached, and handed the stick back. 'I think this is yours,' he said. 'Listen, I've no problem with you tree-huggers, okay? I'm just doing ma job.'

72

'Please,' said George, 'it really was a mistake. I had no idea you were there.'

But the man, who looked genuinely distressed, was not interested in her apologies. He seemed to carry the weight of the world on his shoulders.

'I work for the coonsil,' he said. 'I do as I'm told. I take no pleasure from this, I assure you.'

'Pleasure from what?' George asked. She felt as though she was taking part in a conversation for which she had not been fully briefed.

'I see you've got your letter of possession there?' the man asked.

George looked down and saw the letter she'd grabbed from Anne's hand, sticking out of the pocket where she'd stuffed it. She uncrumpled it and offered it to the despondent Scot, who was holding out his hand for it.

He read it and nodded sadly.

'Have you got I.D.?' he asked. 'Credit card will do.'

Mystified, George fished out her debit card and handed it over.

'Okay,' the man said, nodding. 'It seems you're you.' And, reaching into his own back pocket, he gave her a brown envelope. 'I've got to say, I'm impressed you came all the way up here for this,' he said, looking at her address. 'You could have applied for it by post.'

'What are you doing here?' George asked.

'Doing?' the man asked, stupidly. 'Clearing the forest, of course.'

'*What*?' she asked.

'You're here because of the compulsory purchase order, right? That you got in the post?'

'No,' said George. 'I don't open *all* my post – only the interesting-looking stuff. What comp—'

'The charity lost the case in the high court,' said the man, with a sigh. 'The developers won. We're clearing this forest this weekend – construction on the new development begins on Monday.'

George looked at the envelope in her hand. She teased it open with her teeth, tore the flap back and saw a meagre wad of bills inside.

'That's what you receive, under the order,' said the man.

'It's less than I paid for it,' George observed.

'Welcome to Scotland,' said the man. 'I imagine it'll become a golf course for billionaires, or something. Now,

*Timmy, in the boot, found himself wondering why
exactly humans insisted on trying to live together –
they never even smelled each others' bums.
None of the dogs he knew acted like this.*

if you don't mind, I've got some precious ancient habitats to destroy . . .'

'Woof?' Timmy asked, picking up the stick George had dropped.

She took it from him and flung it, with considerably less energy than before, back in the direction from which they had come. Pocketing the envelope, George noted that its contents would probably just about cover the petrol home.

CHAPTER NINE

Rupert's Secret Tip-off

The car was a considerably quieter and more sombre place on the ride back to London.

That is, for the first few hours, at least, until Julian rummaged at his feet and produced the bottle of Prosecco he'd packed to go with their evening campfire meal. Soon, he and Dick were tucking into it, singing, playing rude word games and proving beyond any doubt that they did indeed know a song that would 'get on your nerves'. George threatened physical violence upon them both with even more intensity than last time, and so they laid off, and merely hummed to themselves.

Then Dick started asking to go to the toilet at every services. The third time this happened, Anne followed him and discovered he wasn't relieving himself at all, but picking up Pokémons he'd spotted. The boys were very much testing their luck, it was agreed, and they were banished into silence for the rest of the trip.

That was until about five hours in, when the eructations of Timmy ('*Why* do you give him pies to eat, George?') caused them to open the windows, which in turn caused a drop in temperature that made Julian put on his jacket.

'Wait a minute,' he said. 'This isn't my jacket.'

'I haven't got a suit jacket,' said Dick. 'It must be yours.'

'Well, it bloody isn't. Look at the cloth – I can't afford this!'

'Maybe it's mine?' asked George.

'No, no, no,' Julian said. 'Oh, my – look at this. Oh, *my*!'

Anne and George could put up with a great deal of whining and fighting and bad smells from the back seats, but, after so many hours of testy boredom on the road, they could not bear curiosity. Yet Julian refused to explain.

'You have to look at it,' he said. 'Stop the car.'

It was around the time to stop for a burger and a coffee, anyhow, and so, at the next services, George pulled in and zoomed into a parking space at an alarming lick.

Perhaps they had already intuited who the owner of the

jacket might be. Either way, there was suddenly something very serious about Julian, so they listened when he said everyone should use the loos and get the food and drink they wanted before discussing what he'd found, to ensure there would be no interruptions.

At last, these operations were completed, and they all settled at a table, showing signs of frank impatience (except for Timmy, who was, to the dismay of everyone but George, feasting on a large sausage roll).

'What the bloody hell is it, then?' George asked.

'Spill the beans,' said Dick, blowing into the froth of his hot chocolate.

'After the debacle of the boat . . .' Julian began.

'The barge,' George said.

'The nothing,' Anne whispered severely, looking over her shoulder. 'We don't talk about that!'

'Yeah,' said Dick, 'apparently the secret service can turn your phone into a surveillance device.'

'Even if it's off,' said George. 'It's terrifying.'

'For pity's sake,' said Julian. He held up his phone. 'Mine's obviously on. And if M.I.-bloody-5 haven't got anything better to do . . .'

He stopped in response to the looks of horror the others were giving him. Then he went on in a quieter voice.

'Fine,' he said. 'After the debacle of what I will henceforth call "Code Name Accidental Barge Destruction", you bloody paranoid idiots, I woke up the next day wearing this jacket. Which is not so dissimilar to mine,' he went on, looking at the lining, 'except, I suppose, it's a couple of hundred quid more upmarket. It seems that, in the excitement, I swapped jackets with our dear, devious master-criminal cousin. And, having delved into the inner pocket for the first time, I found this . . .' He flattened a sheet of paper on the table in front of them.

'So, he's got your jacket, then?' Dick asked. 'He won't be happy about that. Did you leave anything in it?'

'Yes,' said Julian. 'That's seven quid of unclaimed scratch cards I won't see again, I guess. But shut up. *Look*.'

They did so.

They half expected this to be a piece of pointless grandstanding by Julian, which would turn out to be nothing, or a titbit of family gossip, at best. But, having read the piece of paper, they all sipped their drinks, looked pensive, and asked Julian what he thought it meant.

'It's obviously a good property tip-off,' he said. 'An actually *good* one – not like those crap-hole places that he was showing us.'

'The barge wasn't bad, though,' said Dick.

'We *don't mention* Code Name Accidental Barge Destruction, Dick!' whispered Anne.

'Look at the photo, look at the description,' Julian said.

They did. The property was beyond their wildest dreams.

'Look at the *price*.'

'It seems unbelievable,' said Dick.

'It really does,' said George. 'I mean, it's in our price range. Do you think we have a chance?'

'Not only that – it's on our way home,' Julian said. He flourished the *A to Z*. 'Or, at least, it's on the Northumberland coast, which is a relative hop and a skip from where we are.'

'Are you suggesting we go there now?' George asked.

'Certainly, I bloody am. Look at the map – next turn-off, then . . .'

They all watched as Julian and Anne worked out the quickest route there. It was remarkably straightforward – they could be there in less than two hours.

She had purchased a hundred square feet of forest –
scarcely large enough to pitch a tent on.

'But we've not been shown this place,' said George. 'Technically, we don't know it's on the market.'

'Doesn't matter how we found it. We *do* know that it's on the market, it's amazing and it's cheap. Plus,' said Julian, summoning all the eloquence he had gleaned from his expensive private education and three years at Oxford, 'fuck 'em. Squatters' rights!'

George was very much in agreement, but Anne and Dick would never have dared make such a statement. They looked at the picture again, and thought how wonderful it would be to live in such a place. George held up the car keys and jangled them.

'No time to lose,' she said. 'Everyone been to the toilet? Timmy? Dick, got all your Pokémons?'

'Hmm,' he said, looking at his phone. 'Think so.'

'Then grab your damn coffees,' said George.

'And let's cheese it,' said Julian.

'Woof!' said Timmy.

CHAPTER TEN

The Squatting Position

They were on the road only half an hour later. This was because, as they got into the car, Julian pointed out that they had no way of telling if there were any shops at all within miles of their destination, and therefore they had to stock up for an existence in the wild, as well as any group can that has access only to a Costa, a WHSmith and a Burger King.

'Those will not keep,' said Anne, over her shoulder, to Dick, as they accelerated away, 'and they will not reheat.'

Dick looked down at his lap. 'Who said anything about keeping or reheating?' he asked. 'Surely, if I stuff myself now, I'll stand a better chance of survival in the days ahead.'

The others remained quiet on this subject, and only asked George to turn up the music.

'This is GREAT!' said Julian. 'They're called Gorky's Zygotic *what*?'

Dick, meanwhile, was attempting to complete a childhood ambition, which was to eat all the burgers from the Burger King menu in one sitting. He had managed the burger, the cheeseburger, the Whopper, the Double Whopper, all of the Big King except a crescent of crust, and was halfway through the Chicken Supreme Burger when he began to feel full, depressed, sick and stupid.

'Can we stop?' he asked. 'I need to go to the toilet!'

'Let me tell you a story,' Anne said nicely, 'about a young shepherd boy, who once decided to cry wolf . . .'

'Just forty miles to go,' said George.

'Urrrrgh,' said Dick, clutching his stomach, which was (beneath the beautiful melodies of Euros Childs) making the same sound. He tipped his Fisher King Deluxe into the boot for Timmy to take care of.

'Arrrrrrrgh,' growled Timmy, suspiciously, after sniffing it. He left it where it was; then, after snoozing and waking, he took another sniff and wolfed the lot.

*

The intestinal ramifications of Timmy's diet (one motor-way service station sausage roll, one cold Fisher King Deluxe, half a molten sundae, dropped by a child and licked off the grass, and a few exploratory chews of a week-old sparrow corpse) were so intense that the car travelled the last ten miles with all four windows fully down, meaning everyone was shivering with cold when they rounded a hill and the castle came into view.

George slowed, and then pulled into a layby.

'That can't be it,' she said.

'It *is* it,' said Anne, consulting the map for the hundredth time. 'It can't be anything else.'

'It's awesome,' said Dick.

'*Prrrrrp*,' said Timmy.

'Oh, for fuck's sake. Keep driving!' yelled Julian. 'This dog's a bloody W.M.D.!'

George started up and they pootled along at a gentle pace, still casting looks into the distance.

The road afforded a peculiarly handsome view of the property. The sky above them had clouded over, casting the land in shadow. But immediately beyond it was the sea, glimmering in the last light before the sun disappeared behind the Cheviots, leaving the water a smooth and peaceful green, and the horizon glowing handsomely. It was as though the natural world had suddenly decided to pull together for a few moments to make a resoundingly striking advertisement for the Northumberland countryside.

The small castle by the sea's edge was silhouetted against this backdrop with astounding clarity. They had expected to see a next-to-worthless ruin, scarcely more than a pile of bricks, but in this light it winked up at them like a vision from a dark fairy tale. It was certainly larger than they had expected. Whenever a turn of the road brought it back in sight, they could hardly breathe. Although this was also partly due to Timmy's digestive pronouncements.

'How can this be going for just a couple of grand?' asked Dick. 'I mean, it can't be. It looks like it's from *Harry Potter*, or something.'

'Millions of reasons,' said Julian, as they navigated the hill down towards the entrance. 'Heating bills, death duties, inheritance tax, specialist repairs, the replacement of excruciatingly expensive original materials, staff costs, stamp duty, Eton school-fees . . .'

He painted a sad picture of the fortunes of the landed gentry, which made a perfectly convincing explanation for the castle's desuetude, and aroused no sympathy whatsoever from those listening.

'Maybe the previous owner died, the rest of the family lives abroad and there's no market for this sort of property these days. Who truly understands the problems of the ultra posh?'

'Seems incredible, though,' said George, looking up as the car swept beneath the shadow of the building. Their budget really was very low.

They got out of the car and wandered around the outside of the fortress. From each angle, the property, compared with its apparent price, seemed more incongruous. They thought they could make out some stained glass in the windows of the great hall.

Then they spotted an entrance, not far away – double trapdoors, open to the air. They couldn't help but peer in. And, seeing a wooden ladder leading down, they couldn't help but investigate – perhaps because it was in their blood. These open doors seemed to indicate someone had recently been here, or was in the middle of some operation.

'Welcome to Scotland,' said the man. 'I imagine it'll become a golf course for billionaires or something.'

The castle was supposed to be abandoned, so who could that be?

At the bottom of the ladder, they switched on the torch-light function on their phones and looked around. There were boxes nearby which seemed fresh – or, at least, dry and not smeared with mud. They looked closely, and felt a familiar suspicion springing up.

'Why have these been left here?' asked Anne.

'I should have guessed that, if Rupert was involved, it would be underhand . . .' George said.

'This is merchandise,' said Julian. 'All crated up, ready to be – well, here we are, on the coast – smuggled, I guess.'

'What is it?' asked Dick. 'I thought things were normally smuggled *into* England.'

'Who knows, after Brexit?' asked Anne.

'Looks like –' George peered at the label – 'artisanal gin.' She moved on to another box. 'And this is . . . English champagne.' She looked up at the others. 'Is there a market for smuggling that, do you think?'

They shrugged.

'That's what the figure was, on the sheet in Rupert's pocket,' Julian said. 'It's not what this place is going for;

it's the amount he's getting for this shipment falling off the back of a lorry.'

'So, if this place isn't for sale, what are we doing here?' George asked.

'Catching criminals,' said Dick, with conviction. It thrilled Anne's heart to hear him talk this way again.

'We might as well foil Rupert's plans, now we're here,' said Julian. 'After he showed us those rotten houses.'

In the reflected torchlight, George nodded.

'Yes,' said Anne. 'I mean, pretending a photo on the wall was the property itself! Really!'

'Woof!' agreed Timmy.

'Let's phone the coastguard,' said Julian.

And they turned back towards the trapdoor, just in time to see it clang thunderously shut, locking them in.

CHAPTER ELEVEN

Escape

'Woof!' protested Timmy.

'*Ssssh*,' said George. 'We don't know who that is, or whether they did that on purpose or were just closing the doors without realizing we were in here.'

'That's right,' said Anne. 'If it was Rupert – and we're pretty sure Rupert is involved in this, somewhere along the line – he probably wouldn't have been able to resist a little speech telling us about his plan, and how we're just a bunch of interfering kids.'

'Despite the fact I'm nearly thirty,' said Julian. 'Old enough to be a grandfather, in Broken Britain!'

'Leaving the social commentary aside for a sec,' said Dick. 'Does anyone mind if I go into the corner and just do a bit of a poo?'

'Yes!' Julian whispered. 'We fight crime with dignity or we don't do it at all!'

'We must have *some* standards, Dick,' said Anne.

'But no one will know,' Dick complained. 'And my tummy really hurts!'

'Shut up,' George said. 'And turn off your torches, everyone. I think there's some natural light coming through, over here.'

They did so, and found that George was right. They were not standing in a torture dungeon, as they had rather suspected, but in the cellar of a medieval banqueting hall. There were bound to be plenty of ways out. They followed George, and found themselves looking up at the final vestiges of sunset, through an oval brick tunnel.

'It's a coal hole,' said Julian.

'Oh, great. This coat's just been dry cleaned,' said Anne.

'You stay here, then,' said Dick. 'I'll go first . . .'

As Dick scrambled up, they all turned away and covered their mouths and noses to protect themselves from the shower of coal dust and grit that came pouring down behind him. After a suspiciously long pause, given he only had to cover a distance of a few yards, there was a clank of metal and the trapdoors came open again. Dick peered down looking enormously relieved.

'No one about,' he said mysteriously. He held out a hand to help Anne climb back up, and then the others.

From where they were standing, it was only a few yards to the edge of the cliff, and so there they stood, trying to get a signal so they could first find out the number of the coastguard, or the local police, and then phone it. But there was nothing doing.

'I'll try going further along the cliff,' Dick said.

'No, too dangerous,' said George. 'We'll get spotted – the smugglers could be here any minute. And we're too visible, up here on the edge of the cliff. Also, whoever just locked us in, I'll bet they're around the other side of the building, near the car. It's the only sensible place to park, so they're probably sniffing around our vehicle.'

'Oh, God,' said Julian. 'I hope they don't slash the tyres. And after everything we've done to the chassis on that Scottish hill – Lucy Pessell will never speak to me again.'

'Shut up about that, now,' said George. 'Let's go down on to the beach and try to head off in one direction, stay discreet and stick to the shadows. See if we can get a signal.'

'Good plan,' said Anne.

*The road afforded a peculiarly handsome
view of the property.*

They scrambled down the cliff face, which was helpfully broken up by a narrow, winding footpath, and when they got to the beach, they checked their phones. Nothing.

'This way,' said George, leading them along a few yards. They were cautious not to be too visible, and so hid behind any boulder they could find, darting from one to the next.

Suddenly, they heard a roar from somewhere nearby. They jumped for cover, throwing themselves onto the sand behind a rocky outcrop.

'What was that?' asked Anne.

'Sounded like a group of men, cheering,' said Dick. 'It came from up above, I think.'

'What the hell?' said George. None of this seemed to make any sense.

They all looked up and saw that above them was a large overhang of craggy rock, on which much of the castle rested. They must be directly below it. Behind them there were several caves and holes going deep into the rock, down which the shout must have echoed. George wondered how firm the foundations of the castle could be, with this cavernous space below it. But then something else suddenly arrested her.

'Maybe it's the . . . George, what's wrong?' Anne asked. 'And what's that ticking sound?'

George was walking slowly backwards, away from something at the rear of their hiding place. Whatever it was, Anne realized, it must be very serious, as George looked utterly petrified.

As she retreated past Dick, he looked to where she had been lying and saw that some of the sand had been scraped away. At this spot, a curved surface of rusted iron had been exposed, from which extended several rounded metal spikes. These, which Dick and Anne recognized from the many films Julian had made them watch, were of the very distinctive type that belonged to a Second World War-era mine. And one of them had just been depressed by George's left kidney as she landed on it.

Now, Anne and Dick realized what that ticking noise was . . .

They all got to their feet and tiptoed backwards, until they were ten yards clear of the thing, when they turned and ran, Timmy racing ahead of them joyously, thinking it some sort of game.

They did not draw breath until they felt they must be

at a roughly safe distance, when they threw themselves to the sand again.

Nothing happened.

They lay there, panting.

'Woof!' said Timmy, enjoying himself.

'Oh, well,' said Julian, standing and dusting off his knees. 'I was rather under the impression that that thing was about to go o—'

At that moment, he was blown off his feet by a gigantic blast.

CHAPTER TWELVE

All Is Explained

Soon enough the coastguard, police, fire service and ambulance were all at the scene. And, soon after that, Anne, Dick, George and Julian were swathed in blankets, and flashing lights, and questions, and explanations.

It *was* Rupert who had locked them in, but it was far from being on purpose. In fact, he had been doing the rounds to check on the final preparations for a big event that he had personally organized and had been planning for many long months, which was the ceremony for the Estate Agent of the Year Awards. Quite prestigious, it would seem, in estate-agent circles. It turned out that the explosion of a Second World War mine directly beneath the building had caused the collapse of one of the walls and part of the ceiling of the banqueting hall.

'God, and you mean we nearly killed all of them?'

Julian asked. 'We could have got a clean sweep? What a thought! How many casualties?'

'No fatalities,' said the paramedic who had been checking his hearing. 'But there were lots of cuts and bruises, and a concussion or two.'

'So we clobbered a few,' Julian said. 'That's something.'

After a few hours, they were allowed to leave and go home. Over the next few days, the whole story emerged.

What they had thought was a stash of contraband was, in fact, simply spare booze for the bar at the estate agents' bash. And the piece of paper they'd found with the details of the castle and the price tag was not how much it would be to buy, it was the cost of hiring it out *for a night*.

This still left the problem of the five trying to get on the property ladder. There had been many prospective buyers shown round Fanny and Quentin's flat, but they hadn't yet been informed of an offer being accepted. When their doorbell rang, a few weeks later, they feared the worst.

They opened the door tentatively, to find Rupert standing outside. They all blanched, feeling they fully deserved a damn good talking to. But Rupert seemed as carefree and breezy as ever.

'Am I right in thinking you are still desperate to buy a property of your own?' he asked.

They nodded dumbly.

'Come with me,' he said.

They followed him downstairs and outside. When they reached the garages behind the block of flats, he led them to a small space in the far corner, between the garages and the wall. They all stared at him like he was a lunatic.

'I just wanted to say thank you,' Rupert said.

'Thank you?' George asked.

'Yes. After all, I escaped unscathed from that little fracas you created. And I've benefited hugely from it. You see, all the other top estate agents have been knocked out or put in hospital, and they're all caught up suing each other and the Estate Agents' Association for loss of earnings and so on. I've never been so busy – it's a real blue streak. So I looked into matters to see if I could make it up to you guys. And I found this.'

He pointed again at the gap between garage and back wall. It was filled with dead leaves, crisp packets, black

*'Am I right in thinking you are still desperate
to buy a property of your own?' he asked.*

plastic sacks and twigs. There was an inch of brown sludge at the bottom, made up of various unsavoury detritus one did not want to examine too closely.

'This is a cosy, discreet, well-kept secret of a location, absolutely brimming with potential,' he said.

'Don't be stupid, Rupert,' said Julian. 'No one lives, ever has lived, or ever will live, here. What are you talking about?'

'Well, looking over the property, I discovered that, between them, the draughtsmen who made out the plans for these two adjoining properties made an error. The flats next door, built in the thirties, and these ones, built in the sixties, have a slender gap between them. It's never belonged to anyone, and I'm recommending that you purchase the leasehold. You see, the sixties flats in the next block are practically all empty, and, despite the London property prices tagged on them, they're flimsy and ghastly. The whole lot are bound to be pulled down, sooner or later. Developers are probably already circling them like vultures. And when they find you own this sliver of land in between, you'll have them over a barrel, and will be able to ask for whatever price you want.'

'But that's fiendish,' said Anne. Her heart went out to the property developers. And then she realized what she was thinking, and her heart came back again. 'It's . . . it's very *generous* of you, too, Rupert.'

'The least I can do,' said Rupert. 'And this time I really mean it.'

'How is Lily?' Anne asked. She'd been holding back asking after Rupert's daughter, whom she, Julian, Dick and George had looked after for several months the previous summer, and who had won a place in their hearts.

'She's wonderful, thank you,' Rupert said, his smile suddenly gaining an unwonted generosity. 'She speaks of you often. You should see her soon.'

'We'd love to,' she said.

'But, hang on, we're all being turfed out of our place any second,' said George. 'Mummy and Daddy have to sell it.'

'They have to do no such thing,' said Rupert, and suddenly he was the closest they'd ever seen him to being bad tempered. 'I thought that was nonsense when you told me – they're just naïve, and have taken bad advice. I don't want any aunts or uncles or cousins to get into trouble, if

I can prevent it, so I looked into the matter. I found they bought their house in 1973, meaning it's practically gone up tenfold in value. All they had to do was remortgage.'

'Right,' said Julian, who had no idea what remortgaging meant. 'So we're good to stay, paying our current rent?'

'Certainly you are. And, in the meantime, if you buy this little space, which I'm happy to take charge of for you, I thought a certain someone could have a little kennel all of his own. Wouldn't you like that, Timmy?'

'Woof!' said Timmy. 'Woof, woof!'